Today I Wear the Bear Head

Today I Wear *the* Bear Head

Winner of the Press 53 Award for Poetry

Prose Poems

Amanda Chiado

Press 53

Winston-Salem

Press 53, LLC
PO Box 30314
Winston-Salem, NC 27130

First Edition

Copyright © 2026 by Amanda Chiado

All rights reserved, including the right of reproduction in whole or in part in any form except in the case of brief quotations embodied in critical articles or reviews. For permission, contact publisher at editor@press53.com or at the address above.

Cover art, *We All Wear Masks #6*,
Copyright © 2016 by Cody Shibi.
Used by permision of the artist.

Author photograph by Isabella Bozzi

Library of Congress Control Number
2026935928

ISBN 978-1-968783-05-1

For my Mom, two peas in a pod

Acknowledgments

Thank you to these lovely publications that first published these poems, sometimes in other forms or with other titles.

The Account: "Self-Portrait as a Mars Rover" and "The Devil Always Cries After Eating Pie"

Action, Spectacle: "Ode to a Dodgeball Baptism"

Bracken: "Hell & Flowers"

Defunkt: "Be the Roach"

DMQ: "The Lonely Moon Opera"

Eleven Eleven and *The Visible Poetry Project*: "Armor"

Ghost Parachute: "Even as an Airplane"

G-MOB: "Wannabe Heroes"

Gone Lawn: "You Too, Will Be Sacrificed" and "Great Fish"

Hermeneutic Chaos: "The Ventriloquist's Daughter"

Leon: "Crushing on Nerds"

Matter Press: "Pretending Not to Be Dangerous"

Molotov Cocktail: "I Need That Ride"

The Offing: "Thirteen" and "Self-Portrait as a Fish"

Okay Donkey: "They Are Not Dead, They Are Just Dreaming"

Painted Bride Quarterly: "A Dying Exhalation Is Hard to Pronounce" and "The Placentas of Giant Women"

Parley Lit: "Shark Infested Water"

Passengers Journal: "Rolling in the Mask"

Peatsmoke Journal: "Everyone Is Wrong About Worship" and "One Day I Became the Bullet"

The Pinch: "Butterscotch Communion" and "When Your Child Gets Prescribed Prozac"

Pithead Chapel: "Today I Wear the Bear Head" and "Fortune Tellers & Shifting Skulls"

Poetries in English: "Ode to the Virgin Mojito" and "Ode to My Mother's Deviled Eggs"

Porkbelly Press: "Heavy in Metal"

Portland Review: "Imaginary Saints"

Puerto Del Sol: "My Centipede Mother"

Radar: "Gambling Mothers"

Rhino: "The Way Objects Argue Before a Daughter Is Born"

Scapegoat Review: "Nectar"

SHO Journal: "Marilyn Monroe Wants to Listen to the Birds" and "Pumpkin Soup with Van Gogh"

Southeast Review: "Love & Whopper Wrappers" reprinted in *South Dakota Review*

South Florida Poetry Journal: "Baguette"

The Tiny Journal: "It Is Hard to Tell When a Fish Is Crying," "Peace Be with You, Pee-wee Herman" and "Bad Mothering Starts with Sugar and Ends with Salt"

Waxwing: "A Fierce Holy Body" and "My Great Grandmother had the Face of the Beast"

West Trestle: "Long World"

Zoetic Press: Non-Binary Review: "Strong Weak Genes"

Zymbol: "Give Me Skin"

Anthologies

"My Grandmother Had the Face of a Beast," appears in the *Best Microfiction 2026*, eds. Meg Pokrass and Gary Fincke, guest ed. Diane Suess

"Kissing Valerie" and "Coming" appear in *Bodies: A Preservation of Land & Self: A Poetry Anthology,* ed. Ellery Beck (*Beaver Magazine*, 2023)

"Growing a Giant" appeared in *A Constellation of Kisses*, ed. Diane Lockward (Terrapin Press, 2019)

Contents

I. Alternatives to Prayer

II. Sugar Complex

III. Heaven's Fallen Objects

IV. Opening Night

V. Party Favorites

I.

Alternatives to Prayer

Everyone Is Wrong About Worship

I built the world's tallest crying woman. It rained down baptism tears on all who came to lay their worries at her feet. The news called me copycat. The enemies called me witch, and you, what did you call me? You called me treasure. You called me force. You called me beginning gift. You said, "You were that tall when I first saw you eat a double cheeseburger. Everyone is wrong about worship."

Today I Wear the Bear Head

The flesh inside smells like my mother's neck. The world is gauzy and brighter as I gaze out from behind the generous fur. Sweet, ravenous tufts. I hold my roar like a church bell in my belly. My claws are tender sharp. I can't stop tonguing about the honey buzz, the dance of the bees crowning my head. I am somebody's king. I will wear the head until my body calls me home. It's hard to tell at dusk what the darkness will bring.

Rolling the Mask

At night, she rolls her mask into a cigarette and smokes herself. Little fumes, sweet burning whispers through the vents, the odor of spent beauty queens, paper mâché final girls. You sneak to her doorway cracked just enough. Slice of her sad moon mouth lit by infomercials. You're pretty sure she isn't dead. *Unsolved Mysteries* starts with the host's haunted drawl. You try to wake her, "Mom," but are scared of her unmasked face, ready spider eyelashes, fists clenched like fickle peach bombs. You tiptoe away, cold tile electric on your bare feet. You pour a giant bowl of Fruity Pebbles, too much milk, prop up the black and white TV in the darkest corner of your room in the rocking chair where your mother once made you and your brothers hush. Using a toothpick antenna, you watch *The Twilight Zone*, soothed by the singsong sound of your own chewing. You can almost feel it, the difference between characters keeping secrets and those inhaling lies.

Gambling Mothers

Mothers love to play games. A couple of the ones I know are playing *this black widow, that black widow. Face-Up-Now,* and moms down the block play dress up the small dead dream. *Doesn't it look alive?* An oldie ma in the desert plays potato, not hot potato, but a version of solitary root, grows in a bag, begins to ugly, reeks of wanting to go back to a darker world. Still, I Russian doll, play unravel skin because now, I am part of the shell game. It seems like every mother I know ends up alone. Alone. Alone. I can't stop jumping off ships, can't catch me. Tongue all whip for the kiddy kids. Remember when you could make up anything? Two mothers live with me. One is building a puzzled nest of pages from girls' books with broken spines. The other spends all day in handcuffs both cop and robber, conspiracy theories for sale, make an offer. All the other mothers now and gone live inside of me, lighting me up like a pinball machine of grief. The dads don't play games. They are dropping down wells, hiking up electric poles, neck deep in the dark web, looking for engines, tinkering with younger playthings. Scraped and hungry children can't get their voices to register in their daddies' heads. My man can't even hear our children chew and swallow my blood, my bones, my body. This isn't about games, but I am guessing you like dice. I ate a pair once. I keep coming up snake eyes.

Love & Whopper Wrappers

My brothers throw cockroaches in my bathwater, and my father cuts off my braids. All the people who say they love me shove me down hills and spit in my spaghetti. *You were born too beautiful*, my dead mother says. I rip off mask after mask in the morning mirror, looking for the girl who looks like God's fingerprint. I don't have enough money to run away □ besides the next town over is the City of Enemies. I go dumpster-diving for dreamcatchers, and I find a stray dog instead. His bristly coat is covered in sticky Coca-Cola. He doesn't bite me. He cries tears of belonging. He'd thought he would die on a wad of Whopper wrappers. I bring him home and call him Love. I convince everyone he'd been ours all along, but they'd been too busy playing with matches to notice. I warn them, "Love snaps on a dime," but my father has to lose a middle finger before they believe me.

Dressing up as a Bomb Pop

is the first thing I do when I want to feel American. Then I tell myself that I don't belong here and ask the nearest stranger to shame me. I don't call my body my own, and I give away parcels of myself to men in suits. They teach me the right way to pray. I always wear a crown of Roman candles, which shoots out my fizzling dreams, one bottle rocket at a time. Heaven is dissolving. I renounce my womanhood. I unroll my flag-patterned skin. I hold 1,000 crying babies in the great form of my hand. I pretend like freedom is mine. Like in the beginning, I wear a costume of a bomb pop. I melt and stain everything red.

The Placentas of Giant Women

You become a giant woman. The tiny men tremble, remember their tender babyhoods, and get in line in their suits and ties, and flared briefcases to enter you. They want to reinhabit your spent uterus. They say they won't become squatters, won't paint over the dulling crimson and flesh-pink fluttery you have cluttered into the crevices, reclaimed after your children came parading out of you. The men shout in single file on your buttery cellulite, busy with booming stock-trader voices, full of charm. Fever-cheeked babies that want to get warm, be saved, meant to someone. Loved. They say they'll fit neatly. "Just open the doors," they holler. "It's cold out here." They tell you lies covered in hot honey. They say, that at your whim, they'll reenact that vibratory wave that came over you when you first felt your daughter alive in your soft guts, a heaven swell. You know your placenta is a direct line to heaven.

Nectar

For Isabella

Her hair was between my fingertips as she was crowning. I am selfish. I didn't want to share her with the cruel world. Still don't. Her hair twirled, soft tornadoes on the nape of her neck as she slept. Blink. Now she is five, hair to her tailbone, a golden braid that I keep for myself, pinned into a picture box like a dead Monarch, to break me later. From Barbies to curtain bangs. Blink. False lashes and lip gloss. Auburn sun draws down in her highlights. A boy reaches to touch her hair. He is the daggered world of which I am meant to protect her. Of course, she is beautiful, coarse hair in his teenage hands. I see her, slowly floating away, high in a gondola over the beach boardwalk. Eyes on the horizon, they go hand in hand, but first she picks me the biggest flower spring offers, a rose with wavy petals, large as a newborn's tender head. Bursting with the song of nectar, it is soft white and quickly turns fuchsia.

Growing a Giant

For Gianluca

My son stands on the counter, asks to smell all the spices. They say he is small for his age. I hate that we are supposed to grow a giant, that I am a failure, that my womb, my womanhood is the inevitable culprit of any errors in his DNA. Pair this with a Roman father and police officer mother-in-law who has grown a man with *mani d'oro,* golden hands. They want him to have an oxtail as a pacifier, to lift baby weights, to yank his legs to elongate them. I, instead, grow him one sweet embrace at a time, another way he can face the world in strength. I hold him on the counter, let him smell all the spices: sweet basil, deep pepper, spicy chile flake, earthy bay leaf, tangy fennel, tart garlic. I see him growing. I am watching, can hear the slow extension of love settling with the calcium in his bones. I imagine that is how everything begins, with careful attention. I hear his healthy heart, hold his strong hands of gold.

I Need That Ride

Mike Tyson's hot air balloon is made of gold thread, cured spider silks from the rice fields of Indonesia. The strands are harvested in late summer, which gives them their glint and floatability. Mikey did it for his mother, did all of this for her. She wanted to whip around the world twice. She had bad knees, though. Nothing you can do with rickety ol' knee caps. That's how the streets get you, turn your moon pies into skipping stones. "Mama, the balloon is ready," Mikey said. It was a Thursday. The luckiest day of the week, but her knees had turned to lead. She was stuck kneeling at her bedside near a velvet deity. "Come on, Mama." She couldn't rise. Mikey yanked her up, fueled by champion blood, and even wore his gilded belt for grace. Every time he yanked, he heard ripping, her body parting at its weaknesses. "Baby," she said, "the golden threads won't get me home." Just then, in a whoosh, she crumbled from the knees up and the knees down. He lay in the ashes thinking of snow angels on Mt. Hamilton, scooped up the pile with big hands, sweet, spilled sugar. There was a horizon waiting. The great shimmering balloon swayed on his golf course lawn and rose up against the horizon after he slumped into the basket. His mother was falling like breadcrumbs from his pockets.

A Dying Exhalation Is Hard to Pronounce

When I was born, the midwife had a white scarf over her face. Horror has many beginnings. All women in my family have beautiful placentas. My father tried to put mine down the garbage disposal. I thought more of his determination of beauty. My auditory hallucinations smack out the sound of blade against meat. How long has this bloodline been playing speed with the devil? Our ice cream truck plays Christmas songs in the summer. Maybe the driver is my father, drunk and back from the dead. I used to soak myself in alcohol like a pair of used forceps. I am sorry, father, I have decided to slice up the hammered part of your name. I have preserved a piece of all the other versions of my god-body in old jam jars. The screaming sounds like women singing. A dying exhalation is a flick of magic, hard to pronounce. Ha-ha. Ah-ha.

Great Fish

When my dead father sits at my dinner table, I make him cover his eyes. His suit is pressed, too big for his thinned body, gray like my heart. I'm dying for something warm, biscuits and gravy maybe. *Shit on a shingle*, he'd say. He wants to rest his arms, but I won't let him show me his eyes. We will keep him no matter how rigid, his absence of soul, his desire to float. We will not release our fists. We will eat the bread, sopping with salty tears. We are just trying to enjoy my mother's deviled eggs, but his eyes, those lakes full of great fish; they make our stomachs ache like they are full of cocktail swords.

Fortune Tellers & Shifting Skulls

The trouble with babies is that they are fortune tellers, and they aren't afraid to give you bad news. They pull the death card like nobody's business. They rain down knives, and usher in the storms. They've mastered scratching their own eyes out. They battle swaddled like New Mexican breakfast burritos, protecting their golden crown chakras. Their slowly extending bones say, *Shhhh*. We are so detached from God we can't hear the chime of their shifting skulls.

II.

Sugar Complex

Ode to a Dodgeball Baptism

You played scared until you got hit so hard you froze and shattered into a dozen thrifted teacups. Everyone warmed their hands on your dumpster fire. You're a smoke show of crumpled Whopper wrappers. All the bullies dance a cha-cha around your charbroiled effigy and pour orange Fanta on your ball-smacked face with the pimpled holiness of half-cocked priests. While you're wrecked, you dream of your crush dressed in pink like a rainbow sherbet Hi-Chew. She kisses you awake because she likes sweet soda pop, and dummies. You float off toward the door and out the gym with 5,000 helium balloons strapped to your sweaty armpits.

Strong Weak Genes

She lay quiet as an icicle in the trick box before being sawed in half. This is her first memory of shrinking. She waits for the gasp of the audience under the fractured stage light heat. Her brain goes ladybug. The night before, an unassuming guest at her tarot reading asks if she is secretive. "Yes," she says, "so secretive I don't call it secretive. I call it protective." She likes to roll up her money into long cylinders like cigarettes. Can we blame it on the moon today for making her the sign of a crab, walking sideways into life, anticipating danger with her tank chelipeds that hold the world at bay? After her shows, she makes Rice Krispies Treats to tickle her sugar complex. All her masks watch from their pedestals on the red marble kitchen counter. Last night's dream her masks caught fire and one by one, the buttery latex melted onto the counters, but she was too weak to pull the pin out of the fire extinguisher.

Kissing Valerie

My skin used to belong to a woman who had a dozen children, who farmed fields of artichokes. My skin was replaced after an explosion, a hellfire. I started it all by myself with a kindling tiny as baby Jesus's fingernails. My skin belongs to Valerie. Her mother was called Majesty. When I am in Valerie's skin, our memories co-mingle like a pregnant woman who hates the smell of raw beef, the fetus her puppeteer. Valerie was beaten by men who hailed down into her life, so my skin is whole, but well broken in. At night, I touch her body-skin, yanked tight against my organs to hold them in. I tell her how holy she is, even though her soul is a detached light. I roll and splay like a map, tell her again the stories of our skin, our first lesson in kissing.

Pumpkin Soup with Van Gogh

I whispered in the ear he eventually cut off. Van Gogh was nothing like the books say. He had this ravenous style of eating. "Slophouse," he called it. "I like gravy and sauce because it reminds me of paint," he said. At brunch, the hollandaise looks like a dash of buttery sunrise on his upper lip. I told him Everlee was no good for him. She was rumored as a ruiner; dead-crow-in-a-dream-like, but who really listens to a bearded lady. I do embrace my lot of hair prickling from my chin down around my turkey neck. Beauty is in the eyes. I thought Van Gogh loved me because he would often startle me alive from behind corners or in dark rooms. "You could be brilliantly present," he said. Van Gogh liked sex limericks, so I memorized a few for our date, but he ended up crying into his pumpkin soup and leaving me high and dry to pay the tab. I drank his soup riddled with his salty tears. I still remember the used pillowcase smell of his frazzled hair and the moonlit taste of his sadness.

Give Me Skin

My mask is a magnolia where all the children lean. The little white sack offers the clean slate, the thirsty orphan who can sing any song. You can make your mark here; scribe a map that finds where it went wrong. Mommy won't ask, and Daddy won't tell. Tie up the back nice and tight so the mask doesn't fight friendly with the wind, or loosen under a toddler's curious prodding. Your hand peels it all away sometimes, and my face is like morning. You slide on the creamy makeup; you make me feel like water that rushes slowly toward a ledge. Again, you find a way to give me skin. I only want you to see. In the dream, I am a boy on the edge of a steep mountain, and sunlight is pouring onto my forgiven face. If you can hear me through the cool linen, touch my hand. Stare into these eyeholes so that my small hope might bloom.

The Way Objects Argue Before a Daughter Is Born

My bathtub and my nightgown met when I was pregnant, and they fought about how to hold my body. "You need clawed feet to hold a girl inside a woman," Tub says. Nightgown softens her mouth and whispers "gauze, glow, satin, silk, seams and lace." Bathtub is softer filled with milk. Tub says that it collects tears. When I go under, a god's voice electrifies the water, vibrates under my skin. Tub says it floats my clean, fat organs and calls my body great-flesh-boat, not woman. Nightgown holds dreams. She doesn't talk too sunset-soft. They fight loud as curtain, as bed sheet, as death sheet. Tub is angry because it doesn't remember its dreams, and its body cannot soften. Nightgown comforts Tub, and complements its shine and capacity, tells a story to comfort Tub when it drains the oils collected from my body skin. Nightgown says, "Tub, you are a smaller sea. You hold the earth. You carry the flesh. You are generous in your hollowness." Nightgown slides down my arms and armpits and heavy breasts and once more, over my giant belly. "Any day now," Nightgown says, "any day now, from underneath my silken shine, a girl will be born into this world, and held against me, and the fruit-bearing body of her mother, and washed in the tender gleam of you, wide-armed Tub."

Ode to Swimming Through Darkness

Blindness has always come easily to you. Then you are reunited with your mother. She gave you two new glass eyes: fishbowls with betas. They start inside your eyes then swim deep, long, and free through your body caves. You can't drown if you are full of tails and fins and gills. With this sight, you can stop your own predator. If you can lighten yourself enough, there's a sainthood in this type of darkness.

Butterscotch Communion

I was waiting in the doctor's office with an irritable rash on my scalp. There were lots of coughing patients. It started a type of symphony in the long wait. I slid into the soft, germy chair into dreamland. When I woke up, I was bald, and everyone was praying to me on their knees, which was really awkward in that bad doctor's office lighting. I called out for my mother, and they said collectively, "You are the mother." I called out for my father, and they hummed. "Please, the floor is filthy," I said. "Wash us of our sins," they sang. I didn't know what they wanted from me, but I realized I had stopped itching, and my body felt pleasant like the time I'd bathed in milk after being sprayed with mace. I couldn't believe I was crushing on a killer when I could have been a river. I realized I had golden butterscotch candies in my pocket. I passed them out one by one, and everyone unwrapped them like tiny babies, golden gifts that might propel them from their skin. Born again into sweetness. They all curled up like happy shrimp among the crinkly candy wrappers, one at a time, and as they did, my hair sprouted and sprawled down my back and sparked with their dreams. It grew so long it covered them in warmth, and they snored softly. I called them my children and felt full.

The Ventriloquist's Daughter

If you want a yes from her, you must ask her with the mask on. She only wants words through a distorted telescopic face; there, I am a bomb-struck moon in the distance behind all that papier-mâché and grinning. The thought of tenderness makes her stomach turn. She says she can't kiss, or embrace, or be touched. Her skin turns into a chalkboard, and your love is nails. She can let you sit on her lap awhile if you stay real still, then when she remembers that you are a person, that your body is warm, is neither doll nor corpse, she'll shove you off and apologize for all the dead fantasies in her hands, each fairy tale buried by some flaw where a body ruins another body. She is an hourglass of shards, but once I wore the mask and asked her for a kiss. I caught her first thing in the morning, near the window with the most sun. My trapped breath held for any warm light.

Wannabe Heroes

You can smell the cheap hot dogs and oily fries. Teenage sweat weighs down the air. Bumper cars smash. All the girls have big hair, bangs hard and tall as waves on a California shore, the dead girl will never see. Jolene's friends don't know she has a switchblade. She's hidden it in her Aquanet dream. Rumor has it, Jolene did it by the bright Ferris wheel where much of the girl gang planted her first kiss fifty feet in the air. Albuquerque is a starlit quilt smothered by dark clouds that roll in without welcome. Jolene kills the girl by the log ride, where bursts of water droplets float and spatter the onlookers. We don't know enough about anatomy. Two groups of girls are yanking each other's hair out. The blade enters her femoral artery. The circle of girls cheer for the wannabe hero. The dead girl starts with her fists, even gets a first punch in, and has a twenty-dollar bill in her pocket. The dead girl, the dead girl doesn't live very long, and a boy, somewhere, loves her. The dead girl has a name. Michelle smells like cotton candy. That night, she'd won a stuffed bear for her sister.

Long World

Running toward electric lines, soft animals, wired people who ran away, languages were hard to hear without your hands, wind was cold, but full of caws, worlds exploded slowly, falling rocks beneath me breathed deeper and longer. I kept quiet in the long world. I was a warm ghost among the living, my voice a swallowed bird. My heart couldn't stop playing dead. A starlight called me. I kept it.

The Invention of Crying

The trouble with the babies is that they will pick you from a lineup. They can babble their way into a very fine composite sketch. They know you did it, but their fat is formed of forgiveness, so as quickly as they shame you, they want to crawl into your arms. This is how they teach you to sword fight. The clanging of the swords doubles as ecstasy in this poem. At first, babies didn't cry but rang like bells. The tinny sound didn't tug on the heartstrings, so God kept practicing. The babies' cry holds all the sounds that it was before. A foghorn, whistle, firecracker, Augusta wind. You, the suspect, believe that God landed well because you keep coming and tending, and you can't keep your hands off the baby.

Even as an Airplane

My father laughed when he was torn in half, and his mother rushed in with glue and his father—tragedy for hands—used his mouth and could only kiss him. I couldn't thread together my father's two distinctive parts. Our love mushed them together until my father became two soft lumps of pulp. His parents wept and lay around him through the night, as if they were rocks around a pyre. Night whirled around them in the cool cricket air. They prayed by wishing. Sometimes they were content in the grief that my father was torn in half before their eyes—and not in the streets of a city full of strangers who would never try to put a torn man back together. My halved father laughed still, as a glob of shreds. The charm of his voice reached my grandparents, and they spread his remains into a flat sheet that warmed in the glow of morning. My grandparents could watch a mending unending, could, by their blood alone, make a way into togetherness. My grandfather clapped his hands like "I told you so," and my father folded himself into an airplane. My grandmother's smile was a landing strip, wide and welcome. My father ripped through the delicate morning away into a waiting room. He slipped past my daughter's spiraling hair, and wind blew against my face. My father laughed even as an airplane. The horizon spread its wings into the firelight.

III.

Heaven’s Fallen Objects

Imaginary Saints

I didn't know I was a stuntwoman until I woke up broken. My husband said I'd fallen from a skyscraper, my best dive-bomb yet. My children kept vigil at my bedside like tiny monks. I was supplied enough Gatorade to hydrate a rhino. Christmas came and went, and I reveled in being twined in lights, made to sit in the center of the living room as if I'd birthed a Macy's parade. I started to feel my legs again, my brittleness. My family returned to ignoring me. They'd whip by me like a ghost. Their worship free-falling. I threw myself down the stairs on New Year's Eve. Every step offered a snap or a bang. The dog ran over to sniff my smashed face while imaginary saints paraded on my tender bruises.

Another Kind of Sailing

The eyes of the potato adore the sea of black, the soft, silken songs of earthworms wriggling through Mother Earth. Remember when you lay in the mud as a child, transformed by the scent of dirt, unbothered by your black fingernails. You did another kind of sailing then, when you lay on your back and floated while the clouds watched you. They made meaning of your strange shape. How your shadows grew longer, curved with time, and the dark echo of your body knew only transformation, like a lone transcendent root vegetable tucked into a fold, held like an injured bird by a child who loves everything about this world.

When Your Child Gets Prescribed Prozac

Baby elephants suck on their trunk for comfort. I will blanket you with my fingers; grow myself a giant's hand to hold you. I see a shiny mylar balloon lost in the distance. It can't be you. Write your name on passing trains in big orange letters, Orion, so that you can live on through the metal tracks that stitch the world whole. If the cops come knocking for you, I will pull my old invisibility trick. I knew there was a purpose for my magic. You are barely beginning, like today, first sun after winter. The trees are pensively still, holding it in until the weather goes light switch. I make an altar of your tenderness, spread birdseed, and wait. Watch, the eager flocks will meet us there.

Gone

After Chris Berens

They put me in the nest with the blindfold on. The whales are flying because I can hear their swish and moan against the lightbulb clouds. To remember myself, I must close my eyes from time to time and fall backward into the wolves. In the reuniting ritual I lose the white sheet hauntings, send away the bleeding crows, and finish feeding the orbs full of dead destinies. The animals gather around me, their soft fur doesn't save me from the needle. These addictions have faces. I must send them away before I flutter like a dead love note. Underneath my bell-shaped dress, the bony baby fawn wants to hide, but I'm shredding against the light. I can't stop seeing myself gone. I hold the apple like a bomb of hope. My mother's eyes would be the only thing to save me, but her eyes are obsidian.

Bad Mothering Starts with Sugar and Ends with Salt

Don't get therapy so you can be a carnival of repeated mistakes. Keep winning the goldfish that will die in a week and don't teach the children about prayer or proper burial. Grow yourself a cinderblock fence around your heart, the kind that encircled your house on the westside where your mother lived between the ink blotches in books, afraid of who would break in this time. Bad mothering begins with sugar and ends with salt, and don't forget the food so fast the children are transported angrily into adolescence. Provide the right malnutrition. Famish them. Tell them rich lies for dinner. You should be drunk too—on whatever makes you blind. Don't ever listen, not to their heartbeats or tears, or wonderings and god forbid you keep the lie of magic alive. Get them walking quickly, send them out the door into the wastelands. Deadbolt their dreams. Talk about orphans and war, and how many monsters the darkness holds. Remind them how much beasts drool. Never, never let them sleep in your bed because they sleep like sweet-smelling starfish, like big cracker crumbs. Leave a packed bag for them by the door so they never have peace.

The Table That Wasn't Named Heather

I tried to build a boat, but it wanted to be a house. I tried to call it Heather, but it screamed and ran away. When it came back, it wasn't a boat or a house. It was a hot air balloon. "How's the weather?" I screamed upward. "I'm not Heather!" it said. "No, no," I yelled louder. "How is the weather?" Then, a great gust of wind blew away the striped envelope. It looked like a flying circus, like a small, playful monkey was pulling the ropes and heating the burners. I blew a kiss and waved, watched it slip from my sight, and nearly missed the jagged Sandia Mountains. Many years later, a package arrived. It was a hundred fifty pounds. The mailman didn't appreciate it. I pushed it into the house. I gently sliced the seams with open scissors. The box was dusty, had traveled a long way, and I hadn't received a gift since my daughter was born. Inside was a table, same sleekness as the boat, same strength as the house, same vibrant colors as the balloon. I assembled it with my dead father's screwdriver. It didn't wobble a bit. I leaned over onto it with an awkward embrace. We looked less lonely sitting together in the sunny window.

Self-Portrait as Fish

My legs experience their first weather. The fish on the hook wants his freedom; stuck guts swim backward. Someone lays me flat on a silver plate, pulls away tender flesh from thin bone. My hair rises, a fire strike, longer and finer scales, hardening against seascape fates. I'd like to lazily swim against the gritty blue, swirl around those that tolerate me, and never be caught.

Pretending Not to Be Dangerous

My husband says the crabs he catches are filled with the souls of his dead. After the holidays and before spring, it's crabbing season. He leaves like a ghost before dawn, and his clothes are already stained with blood. I draw him near like a homecoming, or a memory I plan to keep. I like that I still feel like I am dreaming. Recently, he has taken to rubbing my legs and feet before he says goodbye and I can see how I am too, a soft animal made of desire. He comes back smelling of the far away, and his ship mates are chummy and tired and manly. They catch their own transgressed souls. He can't kill the crabs right away since they are harboring messages on their hard shells, in their fur kissed mouths, in their pinchers. He treats them fairly, but their sadness is evident when you open the cooler. They lay on each other and look up at the sun when you come near. They pretend, like me, that they are not dangerous. My son wants to keep them but kept is not a thing. It may be the winter that makes us so desperate. The thinning of the veil between here and there. And eventually he eats the messages, covered in butter to smooth the delivery, and his eyes swell up with the tears of the ocean, and we brace ourselves and buoy the dog as the house fills with memory drops. We ride out the rocking waves until Easter, and then he rises from the water dripping, soft and wrinkled as a newborn.

They Aren't Dead, They Are Just Dreaming

At the laundromat, there is an ant infestation. The little legged beauty marks are marching toward a large hole in the wall. I start a load of whites, then get in line with the ants. Upon arriving at the hole, I gaze inside, where I see a newborn baby covered in stickiness. The ants work hard at cleaning the infant, dropping crumbs and water droplets into its mouth. The child looks well-cared for, but I have no children of my own, so I don't know the full extent of rearing a tiny person. A pregnant terminator arrives. "The baby has done its job. Everyone must evacuate." I go next door and buy a pink frosted donut and a bottle of chocolate milk. I watch as they freeze the ants into immobility with ice guns and throw them into large ant farms hoisted onto 18-wheelers. I read a tabloid about the protein-packed insect food of the future until the washer chirps from across the parking lot. The crime scene tape is still whipping in the wind like sweet strands of honey. The ants look dead behind the glass. I am sure they are just dreaming.

Armor

After Matt Dangler

A girl without a father must blow smoke. She must expand to fill her body with invisible noise and puff it out in a wish of fish and company. The dead go dressed as fish. The fish do the girl's will as they twirl in their smoke-skin in soft white serpentine embraces, with their sleepy eyelids and clumsy scales. A girl without her father grows shingles for skin, and must keep a candle burning atop her head, not too near her breakable heart, in the unlikely chance the dead come back and need a point of navigation. She must build a house around her from whatever is available, in this case, the warmth of wooden shards snapped together to form a body cottage around the girl. The protection ensures the girl remains whole, without the shroud; she is her father's girl, the flesh of dreams on the precipice of realization. When a father dies, a girl is never seen again, and other humans only seem to drive loneliness further into the girl's body. A girl doesn't have the words to sift through the mud of death. She can do nothing in her mother's arms but pretend to be alive, stiff and solemn as a log. As the moon shows its imperfect face, the girl blows her smoke in trails of wishing that climb so high she eventually fails to see them anymore. The crickets sing a lullaby, so familiar, in the cool, dark woods where the girl finally lies down and curls into her wooden armor. Her dreams smell of very sweet pipe smoke.

The Fainting Club

The summer you tried to be popular, hot girls showed you how to almost die. *Choke yourself until you faint like a movie star.* Pretend you're pinned by a jock's hands. Try to fight like a girl, but then play dead. Practice your young limp-limbed body against the tree bark, back pressed firm, cheeks blushing. You buzz like a fuzzy channel, hum like a river running. You break character, quietly exhale, dare to peek out. The crop-top girls flop into the young grass, gasping like wannabe lovers, but dry fish instead. They want to find a beach bod god that will let them taste death's ecstasy. You never learned the trick to a pretty, little death. You got kicked out for smelling like heaven.

Coming

Does the corpse flower hate its name, roll its eyes at the popular girls in hallways, blooming their goody bags every period for starboys who only care about skin? "I'm sorry," girls say for their giveaways, blemishes, no-nos. The girl who went missing was found dead. The flower is corpsing. Sing from inception to infinity. Women peak sexually in their forties, a long time coming, then a lab coat studies you in a cold science building, wondering about the fruity smell of death in your flowering. You are a big mouth, watch that in slow-mo, your tongue frame, your gorgeous, delicious and deadly, dying, putrid blooming. An old man waters her too much and another one, too little. Pay attention, I say. Recognize your neglect. Would you like some oxygen? Do you touch the soil to recall the earth of your future embrace? Call forth the leaves and blooms, call forth the familiarity of tongues, long and global. Come here, how you do, with your hands and mouth to exhale into me, balloon me, prayer me, exalt me. Altars are made like this.

Shark Infested Water

The trouble with the babies is that they never did worship you. They are primetime receivers. It's built into their bao bun cheeks and milk-drunk eyes. When they cry, they are calling for the mother shark, who is four hundred years old with tattered and silky skin. The girl wears her mating scars like pearls, a slow phantom sexing the muck. You once listened to the world through the water, its change and shift through a body of time. Only a shark mother would know a baby's qualms. She bares her teeth and rolls back her eyes, thinking of being held like a treasure above her water world. You can't compete with a tiny shark trapped in human skin. The adage confirms the drenched facts: if you can't make a baby happy, put it in the water.

Marilyn Monroe Wants to Listen to the Birds

Marilyn Monroe was pacing the rockery. I was glad she wasn't in the iconic white dress because I'd have to find wind. I was dressed like a messy bed, and my phone was thankfully dead, or I'd otherwise be obligated to my persona, consumerism, and dressing up some Insta-reel. I wanted to touch her hair, but you can't go around giving your hands this type of permission. "I'm paving a walkway," I said. "You?" "Patio," she said. "I want a clear path to heaven," I said. "I want a place to sit and listen to the birds," she said. "I read they only sing when there are no predators around," I said. "I'm lonely," she said. The rain came on quickly, then like a miracle, and we aimed for a thicket like birds do. Her mascara was running, and my wings were wet. Rain makes it all right to cry. We both felt like singing in the pitter-patter.

IV.

Opening Night

A Fierce Holy Body

One late summer afternoon, we help our friends tag their cattle, heifers the color of wet sand. The men holler, clack bells, reveal war calls they'd let die generations ago. Quicker than I had imagined, the old man has new life again, spirited by the fight in the largest girl. The women sit with the children. The damp grass, such a vivid green, it will ruin you. My heart just can't land. Ranching doesn't come naturally to me. I gender the men's behavior. My friend, who owns the land, holds a cool, pail-of-milk expression. I try my best persuasion on the cows. "You're so pretty." I was a bad man in my own right. "Everything is going to be okay." The cows back up against the old fence. You think someone won't take your body, but they do anyway. You just want to get out of the gate. You can see the pasture. You want the confines to scare you free. You want out, to move your grace along careful hills, under the clouds that form dragons that fly so far from this world. A warm mist of rain hushes down. The big girl glistens, a fierce holy body. The last to give up her fight. I turn my back, and the men want cold beer. She charges the gate, slows after her escape, and looks back to confirm we aren't running after her. Whoever watches long enough gets to recount the getaway.

Lava Monster

I became the lava monster and chased you into the grass that had just been watered. It was muddy and you got stuck so I was able to consume you in one viral touch. You melted, like a stick of butter in the microwave. Lava sounds so much like love that we took turns being dangerous.

The Newly Named American Flag Constellation

During the war, I eat crackers in bed until my mouth is a ravaged landscape. The crumbs gather around my body's edges like crime scene chalk. The night I see the bombs like reckless starlight hit what seems a desolate ground on the television screen, I have enough crumbs in my bedsheets to create a sandcastle. I make a tall one with arched entryways, enough rooms to house every hungry child's mouth I'd ever watched make the letter O, and a moat to deter the enemies. On the longest night of winter, my tears become the sea that sweeps me, the sandcastle, and the war out into the furthest point of the water, where everything is equally shipwrecked. The dreamscape of the swells sinks every gun, floats every mother, and rocks the baby boys, dressed like men in fatigues. We float on our fat grief and point hopefully to the newly named American Flag constellation.

Nuns & Dead Gamblers

You seemingly multiply like a holy mystery. Among you, always, little chunks of fatty belief, salty as communion crackers. I've never dared to taste the body of a god, but I have imagined it, dazzling. When it's time, the steam from your pot softens my cheeks and the compass in my gut stops whirling. Heaven's handle is a bean spoon. There you go again with that texture of healing. I chew my thick, homemade buttered tortilla into a halo and place it around my bowl. If my mother had gotten her wish, she'd have become a nun, and my father might still be a dead gambler. Instead, my mother once tasted my Grandma Mary's pot of pinto beans, and her body filled with the tinkling chimes of a music box. She ate the little beans, the little gems that were first sorted by my father's hands like coins for an ice cream truck, or fuses for M-80s. When my mother was full, my father smiled, and she belonged to a future prayer where I was a refrain.

Heavy in Metal

Because my father was said to have heard his father through the clang of the chimes & how he hated the spring wind. Because his father spoke a thousand metal trills into the songbirds' spread wings. Because winter tangled the noisemaker & I couldn't hear my father riding wind through a Van Gogh skyline. Because I couldn't wait for the sounds to visit me. Because a diet heavy in metal is another kind of melody. That is why I swallowed the chimes. All the gusty playthings clanged down my trachea to my guts. I jingled, full again, of my history & potential, my father's stories & my mother's milk. My center quivered with all the mysteries of music. Because I swallowed the chimes. I danced dizzily, dense in the soft breezes that rolled over the hushed hills at dusk. My body sang. Because my father was a song.

The Lonely Moon Opera

The night I stop drinking, I knit a shawl for the moon, the color of space dust. After all, it is alone and pockmarked. My mouth feels lonesome, and water and coffee don't make me float like I am used to. I am on a new moon. I'd never thought of a gun on the moon, how it could propel you instead of exploding a family. Context is everything. Whiskey shots, shoot. The shawl is the size of Rhode Island after a year. My mouth isn't thirsty for the haze anymore. I sing. My opera is called *The Lonely Moon*. I have my star. When I pray about sobriety on opening night, the moon cracks open and white mice fall out of it and into my hands. They are small, fragile, cold, and intelligent. A chorus of them sings hallelujah in the finale.

Thirteen

You shiver like a balloon sent to heaven. The diving board holds you hostage, body a synthesizer, pulses like an unsung oriole. Hot kids scream, shove each other into the deep end. Boys bubble up toward the sun, golden monuments of shredded laughter. You belly flop. Bobby tosses dynamite into the pool. First kiss of the summer, submerged.

My Centipede Mother

I call her Virgin Mary and keep her under my bed. She is good to her young with her prolific arms. Everywhere she travels is a do-si-do. The thing I did not know about the Virgin Mary was that she was carnivorous. She doesn't want to be this way because of what people think of her. She doesn't want you to think of her drinking blood after thinking of her holding her blooming son. My pet centipede likes to crawl around my neck like onyx pearls. On Sundays, she rounds my wrists and ankles, all the places where I might suffer stigmata. I am her largest baby. The child that outgrows its body holds the mother.

The Angry Paper Doll

They just wanted to play with her. Thank goodness she wasn't afraid of paper shredders. They dressed like her, like a Valentine, to be unassuming. They tossed around her underthings like footballs. To try to understand her, they fingered the Bible, where they unleashed the scritta paper Virgin Mary. They ate the Virgin's gentle, deconstructed mouth and mansplained their symbiosis with shotguns. They forgave the angry paper doll for her lack of three-dimensionality. The altars they built of her panties did not impress her. They threw her a body-builder birthday party. They drowned her or taught her how to scuba dive. They lit her on fire or gave her the power of flamethrowing. They crushed her or exposed her to the art of origami. Thanks to them, she had the scars of a life well-lived.

Gut Punch

The trouble with the babies is that they love to fight but can't control their bodies. They thrash in their cribs like upside-down cockroaches. They wriggle like halved worms under a shovel. It is no surprise that they stab you with their eyes and use their thin nails to imitate the great unexpected checkmate, the papercut. They have reason to vibrate like light after their long fall from the heavens. People always talk about the holy beams that will bring us in after death like a magnet toward its mother. We never think about how much the baby's back must ache as she is pulled toward earth, watching the colors of her original home fall away. Landing inside a body feels like a thud, the Original Gut Punch.

Hell & Flowers

My son has a crush on a sad girl. Her charcoal eyeliner a death metal riff; her uncle holding that loaded revolver. My son is too bright to pirouette to her records needled backward. He carries her smile like a blade in his teeth. Her face, an oval opal, holds her shadowy, downturned eyes, a cold river bend. She parts her hair in the middle like the veil between the here and after. If you saw her shoulders, you would know where the world has settled its score. The freckles on her cheeks are always shifting positions, shrapnel constellations. Every time she sings the song of crows, she dances her fingers through a black loop of yarn, making ladders and cradles, and anything like a bridge that can be destroyed with one swift loosening. Her favorite films give life to phantoms. Her favorite stories are like Persephone, both hell and flowers. My son, my son, takes after his father.

Pregnant with a Ghost

The exorcist says we can get rid of the ghost, but I say, "I like her midnight piano concerto." Empathy bombards through the electric veil. It took me a year of sleepless nights to realize the phantoms are returning to the womb state where night wakes and days dream. The world itself is underwater, magnified and magnificent and gurgling. The ghost thinks I am her mother, and my body is her crying room. I have been vacant for so long. I will overconsume banana shakes and teriyaki beef jerky. I offer my apparition every cathedral. Before too long, a necessary transformation will make us both unrecognizable, a type of sunrise. Without the flits inside of my gut, I will be forced to grow wings built from the hunger left behind.

Ode to the Virgin Mojito

You aren't taking the edge off. The people at my table are not statues or dolls, and their aliveness is accentuated by the lack of alcohol soothing my overall observations. Can you offer more? Can't you sing in me loud enough that I become a satellite? Well then, if we are to go into sobriety together, I'll tell you the truth. I feel too much. I tried to buy the website www.overfelt.com and make a career out of this ache in me. My brother told his friend I am a poet. She thought we were extinct. Virgin Mojito, I bet you hate everyone calling you a virgin. Shame is another emoji waiting urgently for all the love. Do you want to swim with me and devirginize the language of freedom? Does your skin want to run? Be my hammock. Be my priest. At least, thank God, you insist on telling me the truth.

V.

Party Favorites

Crushing on Nerds

This is sad. You love dorks. Geeks that smell like pimple cream and have large glasses that make their eyes bob and bulge like silky Betas. You count the pleats on their tan pants and their tight white briefs consume your nightlife. You think about how they must also be afraid of their own bodies, they're embarrassing erections, their sweet-smelling body hair. You daydream about reading the dictionary naked with them, about becoming an expert on obscure sex limericks, or the quality of condom brands. Alex Trebek started it. You blame him for turning you into a quiz. *I'll take dorks with secretly hard bodies for $500,* you think to yourself as Jeremy goes to the board to draw a diagram of a cell in biology. One of his shoes is untied, and he has wax on his braces. His hair is like a sunrise, unburdened and bright. He smells like fabric softener. His mother still keeps him safe, soft, and whole. Maybe it is his mother you love.

You, Too, Will Be Sacrificed

The teenagers encircle me dressed like wolves, rabbits, and lop-sided dogs. I kneel and crush the moss with my bruised knees. The forest swiftly silences when the biggest boy wearing suspenders shows the knife. "If we get a little taste of her, our parents won't hurt us anymore," he says. I am the softest girl at school, easy to slice, but hard to kill. My mother sent me out into the world like recycled angel wings, and when my father exhaled his last breath, I became another dark lullaby. The grizzly waits guard at the edge of the forest. The youngest boy's job is to sing him a song that keeps him growling. Today, he sings a song about the Titanic. *It was sad when that great ship went down.* The gang fills their pockets with forest stones. Then, they place pinball machine quarters around me. I am their silver goddess among the black brush. The girl with the Mickey ears says, "Good thing you wore your red socks so they can identify your beauty." The boy with the owl mask rocks back and forth because he's thirsty for the marrow in my wishbones. The fat suspender-king slaps him on the back of the head. "She belongs to all of us," he says. We can hear the echo of the other children from the block riding their bikes in circles in fits of ice-cream truck laughter. The gang is required to hum in the wake of my rebirth. The boy who sings has a presidential tie. Owl boy shakes his wrist of bells. They start. Before they slice my palms like tart pomegranates, I straighten my pig tails and bury my lips in the coffin of my teeth.

Cuts That Last Forever

Some guests believe you should only have eight forks, but I prefer to gather all the tongues that taste here. Every threshold has a ghost. Our empty blue suede chair boasts a place setting the shape of Tennessee. We pray to Elvis to shine his glow, but he's lost in his broth. We know it's him singing at midnight. *Oh, sweet Priscilla.* The tears that roll down the tree trunk are pink and pearlescent, like the ghost of a song that gets stuck in your head. The heart carved into the bark will ache until the children are grown.

Ode to My Mother's Deviled Eggs

Mom only makes deviled eggs at Christmas. I earned the peeling job of practiced gentleness. My mother is precise in her cutting with a draftsman's touch. The pressure needed from a blade differs between egg and onion. I saw them as a holy trinity. The greenish-yellow yolks, the sweet relish and, my favorite part, the misty dust of paprika. Maybe she'd saved up the food stamps for extra eggs. She was like them, always full of miracles. She says, "I was never gifted at anything." I think of her mother making fried eggs in lard and lies. I always eat too many, enough to cause a stomachache. Before the year is over, I'll forget how delicious and tender they are; how full I can get on my mother's magic alone.

The Devil Always Cries After Eating Pie

The devil was inventing welcome mats when he received a letter. Upon sliding in the opener and ripping the seal, the devil found a recipe card written by his mother for his favorite dessert. Apple pie. He cried when he touched the handwriting because he remembered being slapped. He forgot that he deserved a mother, that matter begets matter. Then, he talked to God about the quality of apple varieties and fed his snake Eve, a large white mouse. He took out the flour, but he had concert tickets to Metallica, so he'd have to be efficient with his time. The honey of the apple is his mother's kiss; the pinched crust the skin at her knuckles; its roundness, the aura of heat falling away from her body. The house was filled with memories, and the devil dressed in black, knowing he would later cry alone. The pie sat on the windowsill to cool while the devil slam danced at the concert. His favorite crow took the first bite of the pie when the sky undressed into night. The air was full of guitar solos, but the devil slept like a baby. When he woke, he ate the pecked-at pie and was disappointed in its sugar content. Always, it can be sweeter.

Don't Fall in Love with the Face You Are Paid to Carry

I was hired to carry a handsome man's face. I was told to walk 75° to the left as if we were hunting. It was like a large ribeye steak, damp with the faint scent of an open wound. I was to keep his eyes facing forward. I held his face with two hands like a loaded gun. It paid well enough for me to buy baby dolls that looked exceptionally real. I was warned not to fall in love with the face. It became a comforting appendage, a night phantom that sang dying-battery lullabies to me like my father did with his slow Bell's palsy mouth. I was fired for kissing the face in the park last spring. In the report, I admitted to Frenching it deeply with an open mouth. It isn't the same now that I only carry my own face around. In one arm, my frown, and in the other, a newborn without a coo.

Be the Roach

I blow out the candles and wish to hear Franz Kafka's voice for the first time in history, and I hear a high violin string that turns into a centipede. His mean father tended that shrill. My father did that too—nights when he was drunk, his pitch would reach the roof, and it would come down like torrential rain. I preferred my mother's voice like Rice Krispies scattering on the tile floor. She would lay a dish towel over my father's chest as he ate so he could dribble if he wanted. My father once broke every single music box in the house. That cacophony seemed fruitful. I scrammed like a roach. Franz Kafka grew even thinner every time he heard, "Every man for himself," "Be a man's man," "Real men don't cry. They cry bullets." On my father's birthday, I bury myself like an earthworm to understand dark women raised by dark men. I hear Franz Kafka's voice, a midnight song that crawls, chirps, and skitters like an undiscovered bug. I, too, am a master at seeking sugar.

Self-Portrait as a Mars Rover

On your sobriety birthday, you dress up as the Mars Rover and sing happy birthday to yourself from the zero percent of a non-alcoholic Corona. Your new body is not as pliable as your test dummy body. You still believe that there is a killer in you. You are the burning star that once dressed as a saturated wish. It is hard to see who loves you when you are floating in undiscovered space. You still believe someone is coming to save you. No one has arms long enough to rip you from your wild ruckus of star-crossed drowning. In new ways, you believe in your loneliness. Your melody sings out from your emotionless throat into the constellations poised in arabesque, and reaches toward & through oblivions for a musical score that explains pain. You wish you had a softer mouth to eat Oreo ice cream cake. You will not always feel like a satellite, sick of yourself.

Heavenly like That

The trouble with the babies is that each version of the ones you were echoes in you like a crying canyon. You are always tending to your former baby selves, and they are just as driven as a sewing needle. You hypnotize them with McDonald's French fries and Nutella-stuffed croissants. These babies won't be subdued by celery. There's a whole detox program for your former baby selves where you submerge them in water for long periods of time until your skin feels all wrinkly and gooey, like the beginning when you did not have to worry about feeding yourself. You're in phase 2 and get to wear a scuba suit and go down deeper and deeper until the pressure in your ears feels like one of the deepest darkest babies is gonna pop. Glued to the bottom of the therapeutic pool is a little scene from the nativity, so while you're pretending you're not drowning, you imagine that the tiniest uncrackable doll, in your Russian doll syndrome, could be worshiped so heavenly like that.

One Day I Became the Bullet

On Monday, I abandoned myself at a gas station on a busy road where I'd likely be abducted or murdered. On Tuesday, I knew I'd find myself again, but that I'd be in another form, like a rhododendron or a pistol. On Wednesday, I woke up a pistol. I was riding shotgun on a man's hip, almost my entire life, waiting for a turn at my future. On Thursday, I wanted my tongue back. On Friday, I wanted to touch something and not only be transferred from the hip to the bedside drawer. On Saturday, I became the bullet, and abandoned myself again, moving fast from hand and pistol and trigger and barrel, and my beloved body. I entered the heart of another man. I was warm until we lay cold together, all Sunday afternoon.

Baguette

In the overfelt world you never stop wearing your wedding ring. There is no human way to sing the song of your body. You keep apologizing in your overfelt bodysuit. There is a blossoming and shedding, all reds and pinks, all body-mist. You are cactus from your birthplace, your father's needled tongue. He drums a hymnal made of curse words to describe his psychologically sophisticated fears. You can't keep up this act any longer. You can hold yourself like a baguette. Unravel this throng of belonging. An overfelt skin is the best way to become a Hallmark movie, an epiphany, your mother's little doll that you once were. Your eyes looked real. You are wrapped in a paper called skin, and you keep coming back to life to touch it. Madame Tussaud says you look uncanny. Your son preaches at sundown with his newly pierced ear, *lay with me, we don't have much time left.* Mother Mary, you keep giving away hearts that never come home. In the overfelt world, you keep unbuttoning your shirt, asking for the choir to touch your scars.

Ode to My Cheeseburger Funeral

At my cheeseburger funeral, the guests wear processed cheese yellow, dill pickle green, cherry tomato red. Only my mother is allowed to dress like matrimony mayonnaise. Everyone brings edible french-fry bouquets. The children wear sesame seed bun-colored berets to honor my service. Leave it to my brothers to stomp on a ketchup packet, pretend its blood and terrify the last of the elderly. My casket is shaped like a golden-brown hot dog bun with that steamy shine. At the gravesite, everyone eats their cheeseburgers bowed in prayer, and they wipe their tears with the cheap napkins. When they finish chewing, they crumple the sonically delicious wrappers. The priest yells, "Yeehaw," as I descend. My crew balls up the yellow wrappers and pummels my casket with the onion-scented paper fists.

My Grandmother Had the Face of a Beast

I never learned to fight, but the beast is in me somewhere. Battle tests storm in, some arrive like a whirlwind of weapons, and others are shattered snail shells. Small destruction has its place. I lost the one fistfight that I was gifted. I bled like a broken fountain pen. I was lost in a series of disconnecting roads that season. I was testing God's plan for me. My mugshot looked like my great-grandmother, who looked like a beast. Surely, she could kick the shit out of the patriarchy, fuck a girl up poem by flower-fisted poem. Under the guard of her dark eyes, she kneaded the focaccia dough like a tentative pacifist. By the clasp of her lips, I can see that her throat held a gravelly song. Her dagger tongue has sliced through time and arrived again in me. Her unapologetic body held the eggs known to grow thick-boned girls, and her hands, her hands, they could hurt you bad, but instead they chose to be the doves born from a top hat.

Peace Be with You, Pee-wee Herman

I put it in reverse and became a cartoon. I can be smashed and reborn. I can explode and get hit by a car and spring back to life. It was a hoot, but then, the cops arrested me for stealing, which I'd only stolen my own body. It was mine after all, but they gave me a felony, and I had to be housed with a clown who cried nonstop because he had no cake make-up. I read to find a way home, and I am sad to say the Bible didn't get me there. I wanted it, the liberation. Please don't jump on the white horse and hang me. I found the neck tattoos had repaired me for the trial, and I could again be propelled from oven to table. In Pee-wee Herman's Big Holiday, they asked him at dinner to say a word, and he said, *Encyclopedia, Pimple,* and *Hairball.* Pray for the holy ability to find the joy in it, that we may keep moving.

Personal Acknowledgments

Thank you to my loving husband Fabio and my children, Isabella and Gianluca, for always being my magic. Thank you to my brothers, Angelo and Haymish, for your creative genius, and to Michael and Cameron for always being proud of me. Thank you to my extended family for the love and connection. I am grateful to my kick-ass friends for always seeing the best in me. Thank you to my super-smart writing communities for your ongoing support. Big shout-out to my mentor, Jose Hernandez Diaz, for your insight and kindness. Thank you to the extraordinarily talented writers who read and blurbed my book. Thank you to California Poets in the Schools for including me in the important work of inspiring young people through poetry. Thank you to the San Benito County Arts Council for the dream job and for continuously investing in my potential. Finally, a huge thank you to Press 53, Tom Lomardo, and Kevin Watson, for seeing my vision for this book.

Amanda Chiado (key-ah-doe) is a writer, poet, teacher, and arts advocate. She holds degrees from the University of New Mexico, California College of the Arts, and Grand Canyon University. Amanda is the author of the chapbooks *Prime Cuts* (Bottlecap Press, 2025) and *Vitiligod: The Ascension of Michael Jackson* (Dancing Girl Press, 2016). Her poetry and fiction have been published in *DMQ Review*, *The Account*, *Southeast Review*, *RHINO*, and others. She is an alumna of the Community of Writers and the Highlights Foundation. Her poetry has been nominated for the Pushcart Prize and Best of the Net. She is the Director of Arts Education at the San Benito County Arts Council, is a California Poet in the Schools, and edits for Jersey Devil Press. She's passionate about birds, horror movies, ballet, magic, and laughter. She lives in Hollister, California, with her husband, son, daughter, and mother. Read more of her work at www.amandachiado.com

www.ingramcontent.com/pod-product-compliance
Lightning Source LLC
LaVergne TN
LVHW051015080826
845145LV00009B/2637

* 9 7 8 1 9 6 8 7 8 3 0 5 1 *